AUNT HILARITY'S BUSTLE

BY
HELEN KETTEMAN

ILLUSTRATED BY
JAMES WARHOLA

SIMON & SCHUSTER BOOKS FOR YOUNG READERS
Published by Simon & Schuster
New York London Toronto Sydney Tokyo Singapore

SIMON & SCHUSTER BOOKS FOR YOUNG READERS
Simon & Schuster Building, Rockefeller Center
1230 Avenue of the Americas, New York, New York 10020.
Text copyright © 1992 by Helen Ketteman.
Illustrations copyright © 1992 by James Warhola.
All rights reserved including the right of reproduction
in whole or in part in any form.
SIMON & SCHUSTER BOOKS FOR YOUNG READERS
is a trademark of Simon & Schuster.
Designed by Vicki Kalajian.
The text of this book is set in 16 pt. Garamond No. 3.
The illustrations were done in pen and ink and watercolor.
Manufactured in the United States of America
10 9 8 7 6 5 4 3 2 1
Library of Congress Cataloging-in-Publication Data
Ketteman, Helen. Aunt Hilarity's bustle / by Helen Ketteman;
illustrated by James Warhola. Summary: Too poor to buy the latest fashion,
Aunt Hilarity tries to make her own bustle several times,
with disastrous results.
[1. Bustles—Fiction.   2. Aunts—Fiction.]
I. Warhola, James, ill.   II. Title.
PZ7.K494Au   1992   [E]—dc20
CIP   91-21989   ISBN 0-671-77861-7

To my Aunt Christine,
Aunt Lorraine and Aunt Mildred,
who didn't have bustles but could have,
with love

—HK

To Joseph Fitzpatrick,
from one of the many
he inspired

—JW

I was just a child when my Aunt Hilarity got the bug to have a bustle. That's one of those padded sit-upons that women in the olden days used to wear when they wanted to look fancy. Aunt Hilarity saw a picture of a bustle in some magazine, and nothing would do but for her to have one.

Now, you have to understand that nobody in Willow Flats had ever heard of such foolishness. The women in town were scandalized, but that just made Aunt Hilarity more determined.

Her poppa had always said that she was just like her Scottish grandaddy, Amos McFee—and he out-stubborned a mule.

Back in those days, all the McFees lived and worked together on a small farm on the outskirts of town; and they were so poor, even mice wouldn't stay in their barn. Since there wasn't any money to buy a bustle, Aunt Hilarity made one herself. Found some material left over from something or other and a needle and thread, and sewed a sack. Then she went out to the barn and stuffed the sack with hay.

The next Sunday, Aunt Hilarity got up early to get ready for church. She came downstairs, sporting that bustle as if she were the queen of England. Her poppa looked as if he wanted to shake her, but her momma held him back.

From the front, Aunt Hilarity looked all right; but as soon as she turned around, she looked like a big old wasp, waving its what'sit in the breeze. Every time she took a step, that bustle wiggled and wobbled as if it were alive.

When she walked into church, the ladies' eyes about popped out of their heads, and the preacher had a time of it quieting everybody down. He finally did, though, and started his sermon.

He was just getting into it when Aunt Hilarity started squirming. Now, back then it wasn't considered polite for a lady to scratch in public, and certainly not in church, so you can imagine how surprised people were when Aunt Hilarity let out a screech.

She danced and scratched and hollered, and finally tore down
the aisle and out the door, flinging hay as she went.

Trouble was, that hay was full of fleas, and pretty soon half of the congregation was hopping and scratching. Finally, the preacher gave up trying to preach and said "Amen." You never saw a church clear out so fast.

Now, something like that would discourage your average person, but Aunt Hilarity was far from average. She washed out that sack and gave it another lick. This time, instead of hay, she stuffed it with some of her poppa's old paint rags. When she came downstairs wearing that bustle under her skirt again, her granny had to hold her momma and poppa back. But she did, and Aunt Hilarity strolled into town for the Thanksgiving Day dinner put on every year by the Willow Flats ladies' auxiliary.

As soon as she arrived, people started buzzing. Some
of them were scared to get too close, since they were
still nursing flea bites from the week before.
After a while, though, things settled down,
and people went on with their eating.

It would have been all right if Aunt Hilarity hadn't backed into that candle; but as soon as she did, those paint rags burst into flame. Why, if it hadn't been for Amos Ledbetter, Aunt Hilarity would have burned to a crisp, padded sit-upon and all. He grabbed the punch bowl and doused Aunt Hilarity good with it. The fire did get put out, and Aunt Hilarity was all right, except that she didn't sit much for the next week or so.

But when Amos sloshed the punch on Aunt Hilarity, he also sloshed a goodly amount on Mrs. Anna Belle Prather, who was head of the ladies' auxiliary and a very proud woman. It was clear that she didn't take kindly to being doused when she dug deep down into a bowl of mashed potatoes and flung a handful at Amos's face.

Trouble was, she had awful aim and hit the mayor's wife instead. Started the biggest food fight Willow Flats had ever had. People still talk about it every Thanksgiving.

Now, you'd think that incident would have cured Aunt Hilarity, but she did take after her old Grandaddy Amos. She put her mind to thinking, determined to make herself a bustle—and make it right this time. With the Willow Flats Christmas Ball coming up, she wanted a bustle more than ever. Trouble was, her sack had burned up, and she'd used all her momma's spare material making it.

When her poppa came home one afternoon with a roll of chicken wire to make a new hen house, Aunt Hilarity's eyes lit up. Pretty soon she was humming and dancing around the house again, getting ready for the Christmas Ball.

The big day arrived, and Aunt Hilarity was ready. When she came downstairs wearing that chicken-wire bustle, her granny and momma and poppa were all ready to jump on her, but her Grandaddy Amos saved her this time. Said she had a lot of spunk, and he liked that in a girl. Aunt Hilarity kissed him on the cheek and went off to the ball.

The townspeople had gotten used to Aunt Hilarity's ways, so when she showed up in a bustle again, they weren't surprised. Of course, some of them steered clear of her, figuring to avoid grief.

The trouble started when Aunt Hilarity was dancing with Johnny Higgins. A piece of twine she'd used to keep that chicken-wire bustle balled up broke, and that bustle started readjusting itself. It's plain lucky the whole thing didn't unwind.

As it was, one jagged corner twanged Aunt Hilarity right in the what'sit. She let out a whoop like a gang of marauding bandits. Some thought it must be Judgment Day, and some still swear a tornado blew through Willow Flats that evening.

What really happened was that Aunt Hilarity took off, tearing through the dance hall until there wasn't a table or a chair left standing. And not many people, either. She spun right out the door, where she slipped on the ice, fell flat on her bustle, and bounced on top of Culpepper's mule hitched to a wagon out front.

That mule started ripping through town, banging into store windows and breaking down doors as he went. All the time, Aunt Hilarity was clinging to his neck for dear life.

Finally, the wagon broke loose, smashing into the middle of MacNair's drugstore and coming to rest. Then that mule started bucking like a rodeo bronco and threw Aunt Hilarity clear up over the water tower.

She came smashing down through the roof of the dance
hall and landed right on top of the town Christmas tree,
which the ladies' auxiliary had spent all week decorating.
The whole thing fell over in a crash, and Aunt Hilarity
tumbled through the branches all the way down.

When it hit the floor, so did
Aunt Hilarity. The tree branches
had softened her fall, so she wasn't
hurt; but when she got up, people
started clapping and pointing and
laughing. She turned around to see
what they were carrying on about,
and she started laughing, too.

Seemed as if half of the limbs on that Christmas tree had broken off and stuck in that chicken-wire bustle. And half of the ornaments, too. She looked like Aunt Hilarity from the front and the town Christmas tree from the back. Everybody liked it so much, they decided that from then on they'd decorate Aunt Hilarity's bustle every year and select one young lady to wear it to the Willow Flats Christmas Ball.

Aunt Hilarity never had much desire for a bustle after that, and I can't say as I blame her; but she always felt mighty proud to have started such a fine tradition in Willow Flats.